The Fox Who Stole The Moon

Grace – To my daughter, Niamh.
N.G.K. – To Kate, Archie and Isla.
©ngkmedia 2022

Illustrated by
Grace Kelly
Written By N.G.K.

There was once a house on the top of a hill,
where everything was quiet and
everything was still.

A little boy looked out at the big bright moon.

"Oh, I love the moon so much," he said,
"I wish I could go there soon."

Outside sat a fox, who listened to every word the boy said.

"I know," smiled the fox, "I could make the boy happy; I'll get him the moon!"

She paused and thought for a moment.

"After all, I am a magical fox," she said.

The boy waved one last goodnight to the moon,
settled into his bed and closed his tired eyes.

"Goodnight, dear moon," he whispered.

"I'll come and see you soon."

While the boy slept soundly in his bed,
the fox rowed her boat out onto the sea.

"After all, I am a magical fox,
with a magical boat," she said.

With one big throw, the fox sent a rope
around the moon.

"Well, that was a good throw," said the
fox with a smile.

"After all, I am a magical fox,
with a magical boat,
and a magical rope," she said.

The fox pulled and pulled with all her might, tugging the moon through the cold dark night.

"Wait, what's that?" asked the boy.

He looked through his window,
and couldn't believe his eyes!

Outside sat a fox, but that wasn't the odd thing,
she was sat by the big, bright shiny moon!

"Oh no!" said the boy, "What have you done? I'm going to be in so much trouble with my mum!"

"I'm sorry," said the fox, "I wanted to do something kind. I heard that you wanted to go to the moon, so I brought the moon to you!"

"Well, that's lovely," said the boy, "but it's not ours to take, we'll have to get it back, before daybreak!"

"Well, I am a magical fox, with a magical boat, and a magical rope," said the fox, "would that help?"

"Yes!" said the boy, "Let's get it back in the sky, right away!"

With a dream and a wish, the boy
pushed the moon back into the sky.

"Fly back up dear moon!" he smiled.

And with that, the moon floated back
into the starry black sky.

"I'd better get home!" said the boy,
"The sun is coming up, quickly let's go!"

"I have to say goodbye now," said the fox, "the sun is coming up, and I'm afraid I am only a magical fox at night."

"Thank you so much," the little boy said, "but I don't want to say goodbye, to such a kind friend!"

"Well," said the fox, "there's something you should know, the harder it is to say goodbye, the luckier we were to say hello."

"I'll remember that," smiled the boy.

The fox smiled back and ran off into the cold night.

While the boy crept back to his bed,
he remembered the words the fox had said.

Because, if a fox can steal the moon, and
then put it back again,

maybe, just maybe, anything is possible.

The night turned to day, and dreams turned to
memories.

"Wake up sleepyhead!" called the boy's mum,
"We're going on our special trip today!"

The boy and his mum walked
through the town.

"Look!" said the boy's mum,

"The moon in the daytime,
what a wonderful sight!"

"I wonder why the moon is up in the daytime?"
asked his mum.

"Well," said the boy, "maybe a fox stole it,
and then put it back again?"

"Let's go and get some tea and cake!" said his mum.

She smiled, held his hand tightly, and the boy forever
remembered the magical night where he'd met,

the magical fox,
with a magical boat,
and a magical rope.

The End.

Grace Kelly runs a small business, Pencil and Grace, where she creates works of art from your photos.

If you'd like to have something personally illustrated by her, please contact:

penciland grace@outlook.com

Or check out her Instagram: @pencilandgrace for more examples of her work.

Other books by NGK:

Harry The Happy Mouse

Harry's Lovely Spring Day

Harry's Spooky Surprise

Harry The Christmas Mouse

Harry Saves The Ocean

Walter The World's Worst Pirate

Tales From Ridgeway Furrow: Save The Stream

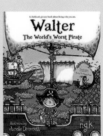

www.ngkmedia.com

Printed in Great Britain
by Amazon

23584730R00021